For Sneedler —S.R.

For Pia and Isabel —G.P.

Library of Congress Cataloging-in-Publication Data
Roche, Suzzy.
Want to be in a band? / by Suzzy Roche ; illustrated by Giselle Potter.
p. cm.
Summary: Describes the hard work, cooperation, and enthusiasm needed to make music and participate in a band.
ISBN 978-0-375-86879-5 (trade) — ISBN 978-0-375-96879-2 (glb)
[1. Bands (Music)—Fiction. 2. Musicians—Fiction. 3. Sisters—Fiction.] I. Potter, Giselle, ill. II. Title.
PZ7.R5863Wan 2013
[E]—dc23
2011023590

The text of this book is set in ITC Serif Gothic Bold.
The illustrations were rendered in watercolor and ink.
Book design by Rachael Cole

MANUFACTURED IN CHINA
10 9 8 7 6 5 4 3 2 1
First Edition

WANT TO BE IN A BAND?

Suzzy Roche & Giselle Potter

schwartz & wade books · new york

Are you one of those kids who likes to make noise? I mean LOTS of noise? KNOCK YOUR SOCKS OFF noise? Then you might be a musician in disguise. You could even be in a band—a country music band or a jazz trio, an orchestra or a marching band. Or what about a rock-and-roll band? I bet you'd like that, right? Well, I can show you how.

First, you'll need two interesting, smart older sisters who can play guitars and sing. Promise to give them all your toys and lollipops for the next year if they start a band. Once they agree, *beg* them to let you be in it too, even though you only know how to play air guitar. Say to them, "I'll take lessons! Teach me what you know."

Right away, you might discover that making music is harder than you thought. Your fingers might get sore as you practice the chords.

"Ouch!" you'll grumble. "I thought this was supposed to be fun." Don't worry, in a while you'll get used to it.

When your sisters play, it will probably sound AMAZING. But when you practice alone in your room, well, your dog (let's call her Blue) might run under the bed. If you start to feel hopeless, take a deep breath, close your eyes and say, "I can do it!" three times. Then (and this is very important) start practicing again.

Slowly you'll begin to like the way you sound—really! Soon you and your sisters will be able to play a whole song together, and then another. And another. You might think you sound as good as the Beatles. You can even pretend that you're George and your sisters are Paul and John—and Blue can be Ringo!

Uh-oh. Singing in public is the next step.

Even though you like to sing when you're by yourself or practicing with your sisters, you may suspect that you have STAGE FRIGHT!

One way to find out is to arrange a concert for your parents. (Don't forget to invite Blue.) When it's your turn to sing, if your arms and legs are shaking and your mother starts sneezing but she doesn't have a cold and your father bites his fingernails even though he's always telling you not to, that's not a good sign.

Maybe Blue can help.

Let her come up to you, wag her tail and lick your toes, and then you'll relax. Later, once she's fallen asleep on your bed, try again, more determined than ever.

When you write your first song, you can call it "I Love Blue." Maybe your second song can be called "I Used to Be Shy."

Now you can let a couple of years go by . . .
(but don't stop practicing).

Do you have a name for your band yet? How about the Thirds, because there are three of you and three notes can form a fantastic musical chord?

Congratulations! The Thirds are ready for their first public performance! Convince your sisters to go to the corner of Thirty-Third Street and Third Avenue to sing on the sidewalk. (I'm not kidding.) Your parents might want to come with you, and by now they'll be your biggest fans. When people stop to listen, you can collect money in a hat.

Eventually, a Very Important Music Business Guy might see you singing on the corner and ask you to play at his Big-Time Music Club.

DO IT! It may turn out that the guy is not as important as he said he is and his club might be a little less than big-time, but if the crowd loves you, it will be a blast *and* you'll make a couple of bucks. (Your parents will love that.)

Don't forget to keep rehearsing. At times it will be annoying to be in a band with your sisters. Once in a while, you might get into an argument.

If you can't agree about which notes to sing and who's going to play what, it will make your music sound strange, maybe like a churning garbage truck. But hey! What an interesting chord you just made. Somebody says it sounds like JAZZ.

Let a couple of years go by . . . but don't stop practicing!
(Oh, and *try* to be gentle with each other. After all, these
are your dear sisters.)

By now you're sure to have fans. You'll start to travel all over, and in every city, from New York to San Francisco to London to Paris, people will know your songs and love to sing along. (A fan might even bring you a homemade strawberry-apricot pie.) They'll ask for your autograph, and newspapers will say how great you are.

You'll probably get cranky carrying your suitcases and guitars, and you'll definitely miss your old friend Blue. Still, remember that this is everything you ever dreamed of and thank your lucky stars.

More years will pass. . . .
(And you will still be practicing, right?)

Remember all those newspapers that said how great you were? Now they might say "THE THIRDS ARE FOR THE BIRDS."

Don't be surprised if it makes you and your sisters feel sort of crummy and sad. Don't let it get you down, though. It just means you're not the Next Big Thing anymore.

You'll still have a zillion fans (well, maybe not a zillion) and they'll still enjoy listening to you. So keep on singing and playing your songs, even if your suitcase feels heavier than ever before, like someone put a bowling ball in it.

By now, Blue may be so old that her fur is gray around her eyes and chin. But she'll still be happy to see you when you come home.

So, let a few more years go by. . . . (And you know what I'm going to say. That's right. Practice!)

Guess what? Now *you're* old! But I bet you'll still be in that band.

Everybody might be wondering how you continue, after all these years, to do those cartwheels and jumps and sing those magical harmonies that ring out across the sky. What's the secret?

Go ahead and tell them. No, it's not the spotlights or the crazy outfits or the autographs or the applause that keeps you playing.

The real secret (and it might almost be hard for you to say) is that you love your sisters very much and you're sure they love you, too—even though sometimes that can take the most practice of all.

Oh, yeah, one last thing. At the end of every show, always remember to turn to your sisters and offer them a smile, then bow to the crowd and say, "Thank you very much, my friends. Good night."